Red Panda's Candy Apples

Ruth Paul

CANDLEWICK PRESS

Red Panda is selling candy apples.

He made them himself.

They are delicious and very sticky.

Rabbit is his first customer.
He gives Red Panda some money.

Red Panda counts the coins
and puts them in a jar.

But Red Panda is sad to give
Rabbit the candy apple.

He is not very good at selling things he would like to eat himself.

Lick. Crackle. Crunch.

Hedgehog is Red Panda's
second customer.

He takes a long time to choose
which candy apple he wants.

Finally he points to the biggest one.

"That one is my favorite,"
says Red Panda sadly.

Red Panda's next customer is Mouse.
Mouse buys a small candy apple
to share with her family.

But the candy apple is
bigger than she is.

Luckily Mouse has brought
a wheelbarrow.

Red Panda's coin jar is filling up!
He treats himself to a candy apple
to celebrate.

Lick. Crackle. Crunch.

Now there is only
one candy apple left.

Duckling and Bushbaby
both want to buy it.
"You could share,"
suggests Red Panda.

But a candy apple has only one stick,
and half a candy apple is no fun.

Duckling and Bushbaby
fight over who will get the
candy apple.

Oh, no!
The coin jar has fallen over!

Bushbaby cries.
Duckling feels bad.
Red Panda cleans up the coins.

"You can have it,"
Duckling says to Bushbaby.

What's this?

Sneaky Red Panda!
He has kept *another*
candy apple aside for himself.

Red Panda sells Duckling
and Bushbaby one candy
apple each.

"Hooray!" shouts Duckling.
"Yay!" squeals Bushbaby.

Lick. Crackle. Crunch.
The candy apples are delicious.

And the coins are very sticky.

First U.S. edition 2014

Library of Congress Catalog Card Number 2013944134
ISBN 978-0-7636-6758-0

14 15 16 17 18 19 CCP 10 9 8 7 6 5 4 3 2 1

Printed in Shenzhen, Guangdong, China

This book was typeset in Godlike.
The illustrations were done in pencil and digital media.

Candlewick Press
99 Dover Street
Somerville, Massachusetts 02144

visit us at www.candlewick.com